PAPERCUTZ™

GRAPHIC NOVELS AVAILABLE FROM PAPERCUT**Z** ™

GARFIELD & Co #1
"FISH TO FRY"

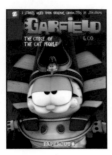

GARFIELD & Co #2
"THE CURSE OF
THE CAT PEOPLE"

GARFIELD & Co #3
"CATZILLA"

GARFIELD & Co #4
"CAROLING CAPERS"

GARFIELD & Co #5
"A GAME OF CAT
AND MOUSE"

GARFIELD & Co #6
"MOTHER GARFIELD"

GARFIELD & Co #7
"HOME FOR THE
HOLIDAYS"

GARFIELD & Co #8
"SECRET AGENT X"

THE GARFIELD SHOW #1
"UNFAIR WEATHER"

THE GARFIELD SHOW #2
"JON'S NIGHT OUT"

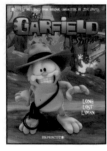

THE GARFIELD SHOW #3
"LONG LOST LYMAN"

THE GARFIELD SHOW #4
"LITTLE TROUBLE IN
BIG CHINA"

COMING SOON:
THE GARFIELD SHOW #5
"FIDO FOOD FELINE"

GARFIELD & Co GRAPHIC NOVELS ARE AVAILABLE IN HARDCOVER ONLY FOR $7.99 EACH.
THE GARFIELD SHOW GRAPHIC NOVELS ARE $7.99 IN PAPERBACK, AND $11.99 IN HARDCOVER EXCEPT
#4 & #5, $12.99 HARDCOVER. AVAILABLE FROM BOOKSELLERS EVERYWHERE.

YOU CAN ALSO ORDER ONLINE FROM PAPERCUTZ.COM OR CALL 1-800-886-1223, MONDAY THROUGH FRIDAY, 9 - 5
EST. MC, VISA, AND AMEX ACCEPTED. TO ORDER BY MAIL, PLEASE ADD $4.00 FOR POSTAGE AND HANDLING FOR
FIRST BOOK ORDERED, $1.00 FOR EACH ADDITIONAL BOOK, AND MAKE CHECK PAYABLE TO NBM PUBLISHING. SEND
TO: PAPERCUTZ, 160 BROADWAY, SUITE 700, EAST WING, NEW YORK, NY 10038.

GARFIELD & Co AND THE GARFIELD SHOW GRAPHIC NOVELS ARE ALSO AVAILABLE WHEREVER E-BOOKS ARE SOLD.

#4 "LITTLE TROUBLE IN BIG CHINA"

BASED ON THE ORIGINAL CHARACTERS CREATED BY

JIM DAVIS

PAPERCUTZ™

NEW YORK

THE GARFIELD SHOW #4 "LITTLE TROUBLE IN BIG CHINA"

CEDRIC MICHIELS - COMICS ADAPTATION
JOE JOHNSON - TRANSLATIONS
TONY ISABELLA - DIALOGUE RESTORATION
JANICE CHIANG - LETTERING
ALEXANDER LU - EDITORIAL INTERN
BETH SCORZATO - PRODUCTION COORDINATOR
MICHAEL PETRANEK - EDITOR
JIM SALICRUP
EDITOR-IN-CHIEF

ISBN: 978-1-62991-068-0 PAPERBACK EDITION
ISBN: 978-1-62991-069-7 HARDCOVER EDITION

PRINTED IN CHINA
DECEMBER 2014 BY O.G. PRINTING PRODUCTIONS, LTD.
UNITS 2 & 3, 5/F, LEMMI CENTRE
50 HOI YUEN ROAD
KWON TONG, KOWLOON

PAPERCUTZ BOOKS MAY BE PURCHASED FOR BUSINESS OR PROMOTIONAL USE. FOR INFORMATION ON
BULK PURCHASES PLEASE CONTACT MACMILLAN CORPORATE AND PREMIUM SALES DEPARTMENT AT
(800) 221-7945 X5442.

DISTRIBUTED BY MACMILLAN
FIRST PAPERCUTZ PRINTING

NERMAL ISN'T **TAKING** THIS TOO WELL.

HE'S BARKING LIKE A DOG IN THERE.

W?

YIP! ROWL!

ALL SEALED.

WOW. PUTTING ON A LITTLE EXTRA WEIGHT, ARE YOU, NERMAL?

AND DON'T FORGET TO SEND ME A POSTCARD.

GARFIELD!

GARFIELD!

UH-OH.

SPEDEX

≥AAAH≤... JUST IN TIME FOR MY AFTERNOON NAP...

GARFIELD, HAVE YOU SEEN ODIE?

WE WERE PLAYING FETCH AND HE JUST DISAPPEARED!

≥ULP!≤

"PUTTING ON A LITTLE WEIGHT?"

ODIE WAS IN THE BOX!

≒HUFF≒

≒HUFF≒

≒HUFF≒

≒HUFF≒

ALL THOSE BOXES... HOW CAN I FIND ODIE AND NERMAL?

WOOF! WOOF!

WOOF!

OKAY, NOT SO HARD...

WOOF!

I'M HAPPY TO SEE YOU, TOO.

YOU'RE IN A LOT OF TROUBLE, GARFIELD! WERE YOU TRYING TO SHIP ME TO ABU DHABI AGAIN?

NOT SO HAPPY TO SEE YOU, NERMAL.

ALL PASSENGERS AND CREW... PREPARE FOR TAKE-OFF.

NOT ABU DHABI THIS TIME.

WE'RE GOING TO CHINA.

CHINA...

HEY, GUYS... WAKE UP. WE'VE LANDED.

I CAN'T BELIEVE I'M ASKING THIS...

...BUT WHERE'S NERMAL?

WOOF WOOF?

I FOUND HIM. HE'S SLEEPING IN THIS SUITCASE!

DOES HE EVEN HAVE TO SNORE CUTE?

ZZZZZZZ
ZZZZZZZ

THE CITY OF SHANGHAI...

YOU ARE LATE, VOLDO!

I AM NOT A PATIENT WOMAN.

HERE IS YOUR STATUE, MADEMOISELLE BELLA...

FRESHLY STOLEN FROM THE NATIONAL MUSEUM...

AT LAST, THE GOLDEN CAT IS MINE!

VOLDO...

THIS ISN'T THE STATUE. IT'S A LIVE KITTEN!

AND WANTING TO STAY THAT WAY.

WHERE... IS... MY... GOLDEN... CAT?!

HUH? BUT HOW... SOMEONE MUST HAVE SWITCHED BAGS ON ME!

THIS LITTLE ONE MUST KNOW SOMETHING ABOUT THIS. I WILL MAKE HIM TELL US EVERYTHING!

THIS GUY DOES KNOW I'M JUST A KITTEN, RIGHT?

CUTE, BUT NOT SO GOOD WITH THE PEOPLE TALK.

IN ANOTHER PART OF SHANGHAI...

WE DON'T HAVE ANY FOOD. JON IS A WORLD AWAY. WE LOST NERMAL. DID I MENTION WE DON'T HAVE ANY FOOD?

MAYBE WE CAN TRADE THIS STATUE FOR SOME LASAGNA.

OOOH... PLEASE GO AWAY. I'M NOT ALLOWED TO FEED STRAY ANIMALS.

QUICK, ODIE. MAKE WITH THE SAD EYES.

OUR NEW PAL DINGBANG IS ONE HECK OF A COOK.

OHOHO! YOU LIKE OUR NOODLES! DID YOU KNOW PASTA WAS INVENTED IN CHINA?

I COULD PROBABLY FORCE DOWN ANOTHER BOWL OR SIX.

I CAN EVEN PAY YOU FOR THEM...

...WITH THIS MAGNIFICENT CAT STATUE.

WOOF!

WOW. THIS LOOKS EXPENSIVE. DO YOU WANT TO SELL IT?

IS THAT THE IDEA?

THERE'S AN ANTIQUE STORE NEARBY. MAYBE THE OWNER WOULD GIVE YOU A GOOD PRICE FOR THIS.

LET'S GO!

AN OCEAN AWAY...

SORRY, JON. I HAVEN'T SEEN GARFIELD, ODIE, OR THAT CUTE ONE.

RINGA RINGA

HELLO?

MY DOG AND A CAT? YOU'VE SEEN THEM?

WHERE DID YOU SEE THEM?

IN CH-CH-- CHINA?!

WELCOME TO OUR NON-STOP FLIGHT TO SHANGHAI.

HERMAN SAID THE BOX WAS MAILED TO SHANGHAI, BUT HOW WILL I FIND THEM?

THAT CITY IS HUGE!

A CAT AND A DOG CREATED HAVOC IN SHANGHAI AIRPORT...

...AND RAN OFF WITH THE LUGGAGE OF BELLA BELLISSIMA.

THE WEALTHY HEIRESS IS OFFERING A LARGE REWARD...

THAT'S THEM!

GARFIELD AND ODIE!

I'LL GO SEE THIS BELLA LADY. MAYBE SHE CAN HELP ME FIND THEM.

LATER THAT NIGHT, THE MOON EMERGES FROM THE CLOUDS...

...AND ITS LIGHT WASHES OVER THE GOLDEN CAT.

LOOK!

THE MOONBEAM IS REFLECTED IN THE STATUE'S EYES.

THERE'S ALSO WRITING: "THE FIRST HALF OF THE KEY TO FUCANGLONG'S TREASURE IS HIDDEN IN THE ANCIENT GARDENS OF SUJO."

IT'S PROJECTING AN IMAGE OF A TIGER HEAD! WHAT DOES THAT MEAN?

SUJO IS CLOSE. WE'LL SEARCH FOR THE KEY TOMORROW.

WOO! TREASURE MAP.

THAT'S KINDA EXCITING.

BUT BELLA'S CATS...

HSSSSS HSSS

...HAVE BEEN LISTENING.

YA!

IT OPENS A SECRET COMPARTMENT!

CLICK

IT'S A GOLDEN MEDALLION!

IT SAYS THIS IS HALF OF THE MEDALLION THAT IS THE KEY TO THE TREASURE OF FUCANGLONG.

THE OTHER HALF IS HELD BY THE OLD MASTER OF THE TEMPLE ON MOUNT QINGSHAN!

THAT'S KIND OF FAR.

IS THERE A FOOD TRUCK THAT GOES THAT WAY?

WE WILL NEED TO FIND TRANSPORTATION.

I RECOGNIZE THAT LOOK, MY FRIEND.

WE CAN STOP FOR LUNCH.

HSSSSSS
HSSS

LATER...

THANK YOU FOR THE DINNER AND FOR YOUR LESSONS.

HOW MUCH LONGER BEFORE WE ARE WORTHY OF THE MEDALLION'S OTHER HALF?

BEST CHINESE FOOD EVER. IF WE GET HOME, I WONDER IF HE'LL DELIVER TO OUR NEIGHBORHOOD?

I HAVE BEEN OBSERVING YOU.

EXCEPT FOR DINGBANG, YOU ARE THE WORST STUDENTS I HAVE EVER HAD.

BUT YOU HAVE GOOD HEARTS AND YOU ARE LOYAL FRIENDS.

MORE OR LESS.

THEREFORE, YOU HAVE EARNED MY HALF OF THE MEDALLION.

THANK YOU!

YOU HONOR US. NOW WE HAVE THE COMPLETE KEY.

SNAP

ACCORDING TO LEGEND...

...STARE NOT INTO THE EYE OF FUCANGLONG.

IT HAS DEFEATED ENTIRE ARMIES.

HEY...

THE STATUE IS PROJECTING THE IMAGE OF A TIGER.

I UNDERSTAND WHAT THE TIGER REPRESENTS...

IT'S TIGER VALLEY NEAR BEIJING, RIGHT BY THE GREAT WALL OF CHINA!

THE TREASURE IS THERE!

LET'S GO, MY FRIENDS.

GOOD LUCK, MY STUDENTS. YOU WILL NEED IT.

THANK YOU, OLD MASTER.

HSSSSS
HSSS

SHANGHAI...

UH, EXCUSE ME...

I'M LOOKING FOR BELLA BELLISSIMA.

I'M THE OWNER OF THE DOG AND CAT WHO TOOK YOUR SUITCASE.

HAS ANYONE FOUND THEM YET?

YOU'RE JUST IN TIME! THESE ANIMALS... THEY ARE VERY IMPORTANT TO YOU, YES?

OF COURSE!

AND YOU MUST BE VERY IMPORTANT TO THEM.

YES!

PLEASE WAIT IN THIS ROOM.

SLAM

WE'LL BE BRINGING YOU TO YOUR BELOVED PETS SHORTLY. WE JUST HAVE TO MAKE A FEW ARRANGEMENTS.

SO SIT TIGHT AND ENJOY THE COMPLIMENTARY DRINKS AND SNACKS.

BAM BAM BAM

LET ME OUT!

MISS BELLA! WE HAVE THE GPS SIGNAL FROM THE COLLARS OF YOUR CATS!

THEY'RE HEADING TOWARDS TIGER VALLEY!

LET'S GO. BRING THE AMERICAN!

29

the GARFIELD show
FAME FATALE

ODIE. LOOK. THEY'RE TALKING ABOUT LEONARDO ON THE TV.

LEONARDO IS ONE OF HOLLYWOOD'S HOTTEST STARS, BUT WHY IS HE SO SAD?

LEONARDO HAS BEEN UNDER A GREAT DEAL OF STRESS. PAPARAZZI AND REPORTERS TAIL HIM DAY AND NIGHT!

HE NEEDS SOME REST BEFORE HE STARS IN HIS NEXT MOVIE.

÷PFF!÷... SOME PEOPLE HAVE REAL PROBLEMS. MY REMOTE CONTROL IS BROKEN, BUT DO YOU HEAR ME COMPLAIN?

TURN IT OFF, WILL YOU, ODIE?

WOOF!

THAT'S THE CAR. JON IS BACK, BUT WHAT IS HE--

HUH?

QUICK! LET'S HURRY INSIDE!

IT'S ALL CLEAR, LIZ. I DON'T THINK ANYONE SAW US.

YOU LOOK LIKE YOU JUST ROBBED A BANK.

WHAT ARE YOU HIDING UNDER THERE?

GARFIELD, ODIE, MEET LEONARDO!

LIZ IS HIS VETERINARIAN. SHE THOUGHT OUR HOUSE WOULD BE A QUIET PLACE FOR HIM TO GET AWAY FROM THE PRESS AND REST.

HELLO!

WOW. A BIG STAR AT OUR HOUSE.

COME ON, STAR, I'LL SHOW YOU AROUND. YOU HUNGRY?

I'M FAMISHED!

HMM... IF I MAY ASK... WHAT EXACTLY ARE THESE?

IF YOU HAVE TO ASK... FISH STICKS.

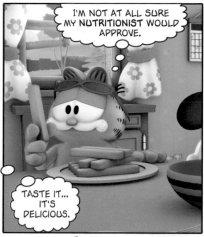

I'M NOT AT ALL SURE MY NUTRITIONIST WOULD APPROVE.

TASTE IT... IT'S DELICIOUS.

YUMMY! THESE ARE REALLY GOOD!

LEONARDO LEONARDO LEONARDO LEONARDO LEONARDO

NO! THEY'VE FOUND ME! THE FANS AND THE PRESS HAVE FOUND ME!

REPORTS OF BANK ROBBERS IN A QUIET NEIGHBORHOOD HAVE, INSTEAD, EXPOSED THE HIDING PLACE OF INTERNATIONAL STAR LEONARDO!

IT'S A MOB OUT THERE. HOW DID THEY FIND YOU?

≥SIGH.≤ THEY ALWAYS DO. TIME TO FACE MY PUBLIC AGAIN.

HOLD UP A SECOND...

LEONARDO CAME OUT OF HIDING TODAY, SIGNING AUTOGRAPHS AND POSING WITH DOZENS OF HIS FANS AT THE HOME OF A FRIEND.

DESPITE RUMORS OF HIS BEING EXHAUSTED, SIR LEO WAS IN TOP FORM AS HE CHARMED THE CROWD AND THIS REPORTER.

BRILLIANT! YOU, SIR, MAKE A BETTER LEONARDO THAN I DO!

SO... WHEN DO I GET TO RIDE IN YOUR LIMOUSINE?

IN ABOUT TEN MINUTES. YOU CAN FILL IN FOR ME ALL DAY!

LEONARDO LEONARDO LEONARDO LEONARDO LEONARDO LEONARDO

FLASH
FLASH

I HOPE HE HAS A GOOD TIME BEING ME.

I KNOW I'LL ENJOY MY NAP.

VROOOM

SOUNDS LIKE FUN. HOW MUCH WORK CAN THAT BE?

HMM... YOU'VE GAINED SOME WEIGHT. WE'LL TALK DIET LATER.

VACATION OR NOT, YOU COULDN'T PASS UP THIS COMMERCIAL.

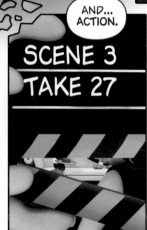

AND... ACTION.

SCENE 3
TAKE 27

IF YOU TRULY LOVE YOUR PET, CAT-VIAR PUTS THE CAT IN CAVIAR!

MEEEOOW!

FINALLY! THAT'S A WRAP!

TO THE MOVIE THEATER AND STEP ON IT! WE CAN'T BE LATE FOR LEONARDO'S OWN PREMIERE!

LEONARDO LEONARDO LEONARDO LEONARDO LEONARDO

FLASH FLASH FLASH FLASH FLASH

04:1
06:20
08:15
10:30

MUST... HAVE... POPCORN!

ADRIAN SLANDER HERE WITH THE SHOCKING NEWS THAT LEONARDO, THE STAR OF "THE DEVERMINATOR," IS ACTUALLY FRIENDS WITH RODENTS!

A SWARM OF SIR LEO'S MOUSY FRIENDS ATTACKED FANS AND REPORTERS OUTSIDE HIS TEMPORARY HOME.

WHAT?!

IS THIS THE END OF HIS CAREER?

ME? A FRIEND OF MICE?!

I'D NEVER DARE SHOW MY FACE IN HOLLYWOOD AGAIN!

I THINK YOU MEAN "MY" FACE SINCE YOU SWITCHED LIVES WITH ME.

OKAY, OKAY, I GET IT.

YOU CAN HAVE YOUR LIFE BACK!

BUT YOU HAVE TO HELP ME GET OUT OF THIS MESS...

...BEFORE I END UP DOING "REALITY" TV SHOWS.

MY FRIEND NERMAL

46

HI, NERMAL.

GARFIELD?!

LOOK WHAT WE GOT HERE, BOYS! TWO CATS TO... HEH... PLAY WITH.

ABOUT THAT...

SCRATCH SCRATCH

HUH?

BOTH OF US ARE INFESTED WITH MONGOLIAN MONSTER FLEAS.

SCRATCH SCRATCH

SO VERY CONTAGIOUS.

SCRATCH SCRATCH

FOLLOW MY LEAD, KID.

SCRATCH

SCRATCH

SCRATCH

SCRATCH

SCRATCH

÷OOP.÷ ÷UGH.÷ ÷EEK÷ ÷AGH.÷

THE CUTE ONE LOOKS REALLY INFESTED.

THE FAT ONE SAID THEY WERE VERY CONTAGIOUS.

RUN AWAY! RUN AWAY!

LATER...

I'LL DO THE HOUSEWORK FOR MY FRIEND, GARFIELD.

RUUMMMM

WHAT'S GOING ON IN THE LIVING ROOM?

NERMAL! YOU HAVE THE VACUUM CLEANER SET TOO HIGH!

MY ICE CREAM!

RRRUUUUMMMM

TURN THAT CRAZY THING OFF!

MMMMMMMMM

WAIT, GARFIELD. I CAN'T HEAR YOU.

I'LL TURN THE VACUUM OFF.

RRRUUUUUMMMMMMMMMMMMMMMN

YOU TURNED IT UP TO SUPER-SUCTION!

DON'T TRY TO BLAME THIS DISASTER ON CUTE LITTLE NERMAL!

I'LL HAVE TO STRAIGHTEN EVERYTHING UP MYSELF.

I WANT YOU OUTSIDE RIGHT NOW!

≳GRRRRR!≲

I WAS JUST TRYING TO HELP YOU.

HEY...

HERE'S ANOTHER FRIEND OF MINE. YOU'LL LIKE HER.

SO THIS IS YOUR BIG STRONG HERO...

HE'S THE FATTEST, ERR, BIGGEST HERO IN THE NEIGHBORHOOD!

≳PURR.≲ I'VE ALWAYS WANTED TO BE RESCUED BY A BIG STRONG HERO.

AH... I... ERR...

TAP TAP TAP

52

LATER, DURING A RARE MOMENT WHEN NERMAL'S NOT AROUND...

GRRRRR

MAYBE I SHOULD'VE THOUGHT THIS PLAN THROUGH.

COULD YOU GIVE ME JUST ANOTHER MINUTE?

GRRRR

VERY PAINFUL THESE MONGOLIAN MONSTER FLEAS...

GRRRRR

SCRATCH

SCRATCH

SCRATCH
SCRATCH

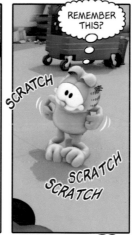

REMEMBER THIS?

SCRATCH

SCRATCH
SCRATCH

AND CONTAGIOUS LIKE CRAZY...

SCRATCH

SCRATCH

SCRATCH

WE'RE NOT THE LEAST BIT WORRIED, CAT.

WE'RE WEARING OUR NEW FLEA COLLARS.

UH-OH...

LIFE FLASHING BEFORE MY EYES AGAIN.

FAREWELL, LASAGNA...

OKAY, GUYS! LET'S HAVE SOME FUN OUT HERE!

I HAVE A FULL DAY PLANNED FOR INSIDE... LIKE COUNTING ALL THE WAYS I HATE THE COLD AND THE SNOW.

YIPPEEEE

AAAAAAA AA AA A A A A

WE'LL CATCH SOME FISH FOR TONIGHT'S DINNER.

I WANT TO BUILD A SNOWMAN. I'LL CALL HIM BORIS.

GARFIELD! COME LOOK!

GRUMBLE!

IT'S A VERY NICE SNOWMAN. DOES IT COME WITH A PIZZA?

DON'T WORRY. WE WENT FISHING FOR OUR DINNER.

LET'S DIG IN!

YOU WENT FISHING AND YOU CAUGHT CANNED SPINACH?

IT'S DELICIOUS CANNED SPINACH.

FOR SHIPPING FROZEN FOODS, ALWAYS THINK "FRIGOPOST®"!

IN OTHER NEWS, TONIGHT MARS, VENUS, AND JUPITER ALIGN WITH EARTH. COSMIC RAYS--

COULD SOME REAL FOOD ALIGN WITH MY STOMACH?

GOOD NIGHT, GARFIELD AND ODIE AND BORIS.

ZZZZZZ ZZZZ ZZZ

ZZZZZZZ

WOOF WOOF!

ODIE! WHY ALL THE BARKING?

WOOF WOOF!

WHAT? BORIS THE SNOWMAN IS GONE?

BUT THAT'S IMPOSSIBLE.

WOOF WOOF!

≑SIGH.≑ I'LL GO OUTSIDE WITH YOU.

BORIS IS GONE AND THERE ARE TRACKS IN THE SNOW.

IT WOULD BE REALLY DUMB...

...TO FOLLOW THESE TRACKS INTO THE NIGHT.

DID WE LEARN NOTHING FROM HORROR MOVIES?

HEY, OLAF, HOW DO YOU KNOW WHEN A SNOWMAN IS SAD?

AND NOW WE'RE HEARING VOICES.

I DON'T KNOW, BORIS, HOW?

WHEN YOU SEE HIM CRY ICE CUBES!

HA HA HA! THAT'S COLD, BROTHER.

GOT ANY MORE?

AH... HELLO? YOU...

YOU'RE REALLY TALKING?

OF COURSE!

IT'S CLASSIC REALLY. THREE PLANETS ALIGN WITH EARTH. WE GET HIT WITH COSMIC RAYS. NOW WE'RE ALIVE. JUST ROLL WITH IT.

NOW THAT YOU KNOW OUR SECRET, WHY NOT GET IN ON THE FUN?

OKAY. WHAT DO SNOWMEN CALL SNOWBALLS?

"CHILDREN."

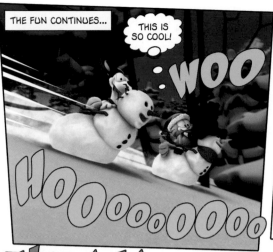

THE FUN CONTINUES... THIS IS SO COOL!

WOO

HOOoooOOOo

SNOWBALL FIGHT!

AND SO THE DAYS PASS...

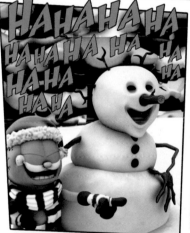

HAHAHAHA HAHAHA HA HA HA HAHA HAHA

I'VE GOT A GOOD HEAD FOR JUGGLING!

WHAT A WEEK. WE HAD A GREAT TIME.

I'M ACTUALLY SORRY OUR TRIP IS OVER.

BUT WE'LL SEE YOU AGAIN NEXT YEAR.

I'M AFRAID NOT. THE TEMPERATURE'S RISING.

WE'LL START MELTING SOON.

NO! WE CAN'T HAVE A SAD ENDING TO THIS STORY.

I HAVE AN IDEA!

FRIGOPOST®!

61

SOME TIME LATER...

WE GOT A POSTCARD.

IT'S FROM OUR SNOWMAN FRIENDS...

WOOF?

"DEAR ODIE AND GARFIELD...

"IT'S FREEZING UP HERE AT THE NORTH POLE AND WE LOVE IT!

"YOU GUYS SHOULD VISIT US SOMETIME. WE PROMISE YOU A WARM RECEPTION. BUT NOT TOO WARM. COOLLY YOURS, BORIS AND OLAF"

DON'T YOU JUST LOVE A HAPPY ENDING?

THIS CALLS FOR ICE CREAM.

THE END

WATCH OUT FOR PAPERCUTZ™

Welcome to the fabulously furry fourth THE GARFIELD SHOW graphic novel from Papercutz, the cat-loving folks devoted to publishing great graphic novels for all ages. I'm Jim Salicrup, Editor-in-Chief and fellow lasagna aficionado, here to talk about a few other cartoon cats, cats we like to call THE PAPERCATZ…

While Garfield is certainly Top Cat, so to speak, at Papercutz, there certainly are a few other cartoon kitties populating the pages of several other Papercutz publications. You may even remember some of them from the quirky quiz we ran back in THE GARFIELD SHOW #2.

The first is fairly well-known, as the pet of Gargamel, the evil wizard obsessed with making life difficult for our little blue buddies, THE SMURFS. Of course, we're talking about Azrael, perhaps the oldest cat currently running in our graphic novels. The Smurfs were created over 50 years ago by Pierre Culliford, better known as Peyo, and Azrael debuted right alongside Gargamel in the very first panel of "The Smurfnapper." Azrael isn't necessarily a bad cat, as I believe most cats would want to attack Smurfs if given the opportunity. Just like we can't choose our parents, Azrael didn't choose gargamel to be his owner. You can find this story in both THE SMURFS #9 "Gargamel and the Smurfs" and the first volume of the deluxe THE SMURFS ANTHOLOGY.

Believing in equal time, believe it or not, Papercutz actually publishes a couple of titles starring… mice! Yes, it's true. In GERONIMO STILTON, the adventures of the time-travelling Editor-in-Chief of New Mouse City's The Rodent's Gazette, who is perpetually saving the future, by protecting the past, the villains are the wicked Pirate Cats—Catardone III of Catatonia, Tersilla of catatonia, and Bonzo Felix (Yes, a cat named Felix!). Unlike Garfield, who long ago gave up the notion of battling mice, The Pirate Cats continually persist in trying to get the upper paw in their dealings with Geronimo and his family and friends. They even go so far as to disguise themselves as mice, but it's all to no avail. They never win.

For the overly literal of you, you may be asking if Papercutz publishes two titles starring mice (GERONIMO STILTON and THEA STILTON) and only one starring a cat, how is that "equal time." Well, it's not. But we will soon be publishing another book by Peyo entitled PUSSYCAT, which will collect all of his cat comic strips in one volume. This cat actually came before Azrael, so he will soon be the oldest Papercutz cat. These strips have never before been collected or published in America until now. If you're curious, like a cat, and want to see the early work of the cartoonist who created THE SMURFS, this book is for you!

There are actually several more cats appearing in other Papercutz graphic novels, but we're actually running out of room, so maybe we should save the rest for THE GARFIELD SHOW #5?

Speaking of which, for those fans of great comicbook lettering are wondering what happened to Tom Orzechowski (I said he'd be back in this book), he had to take some time off to move from California to Ohio. He'll be back in THE GARFIELD SHOW #5, but we wanted to thank the wonderful Janice Chiang for filling in for him! So, let's all do this again (except you, Janice), when we return in THE GARFIELD SHOW #5!

Thanks,

Jim

STAY IN TOUCH!

EMAIL: SALICRUP@PAPERCUTZ.COM
WEB: PAPERCUTZ.COM
TWITTER: @PAPERCUTZGN
FACEBOOK: PAPERCUTZGRAPHICNOVELS
BIRTHDAY CARDS: PAPERCUTZ, 160 BROADWAY, SUITE 700, EAST WING, NEW YORK, NY 10038

More Great Graphic Novels from PAPERCUTZ™

DISNEY FAIRIES #15

"Tinker Bell and the Secret of the Wings"

The hit DVD in comics!

ERNEST & REBECCA #5

"The School of Nonsense"

A 6 ½ year old girl and her microbial buddy against the world!

MIGHTY MORPHIN POWER RANGERS #2

"Going Green"

The Green Ranger's origins: revealed!

RIO #1

"Snakes Alive!"

An all-new, exclusive prequel to RIO 2 that takes place after the original hit RIO film!

THE SMURFS #18

"The Smurf Accountant"

More money, more problems in the Smurf's Village!

SYBIL THE BACKPACK FAIRY #4

"Princess Nina"

Nina and Sybil's Excellent Adventure Through Time!

Available at better booksellers everywhere!

Or order directly from us! DISNEY FAIRIES is available in paperback for $7.99, in hardcover for $11.99; ERNEST & REBECCA is $11.99 in hardcover only; MIGHTY MORPHIN POWER RANGERS is available in paperback for $7.99, in hardcover for $12.99; RIO is available in paperback for $7.99 each, in hardcover for $11.99; THE SMURFS are available in paperback for $5.99, in hardcover for $10.99; and SYBIL THE BACKPACK FAIRY is available in hardcover only for $10.99.

Please add $4.00 for postage and handling for the first book, add $1.00 for each additional book.

Please make check payable to NBM Publishing. Send to: PAPERCUTZ, 160 Broadway, Suite 700, East Wing, New York, NY 10038

(1-800-886-1223)